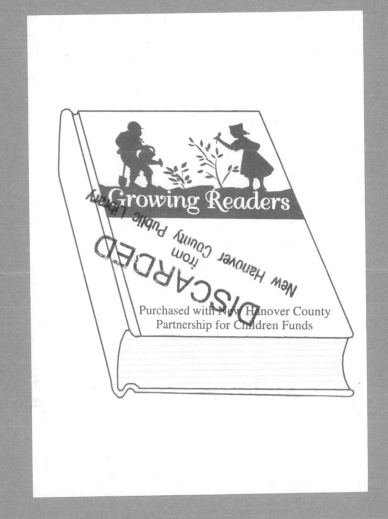

DUCKLINGS AND POLLYWOGS

by **Anne Rockwell**

illustrated by **Lizzy Rockwell**

Macmillan Publishing Company   New York   Maxwell Macmillan Canada   Toronto

Maxwell Macmillan International   New York   Oxford   Singapore   Sydney

For Nicholas and Nigel

Library of Congress Cataloging-in-Publication Data. Rockwell, Anne F. Ducklings and pollywogs / by Anne Rockwell ; illustrated by Lizzy Rockwell. — 1st ed.   p.   cm. Summary: A little girl and her father watch the changes that take place at a pond in the woods during each season. ISBN 0-02-777452-X   [1. Ponds—Fiction. 2. Seasons—Fiction. 3. Fathers and daughters—Fiction.] I. Rockwell, Lizzy, ill. II. Title. PZ7.R5943Du 1994   [E]—dc20   93-16600

In winter, lots of people went
to the woods to skate
on the ice on the pond.

But when the ice melted,
my father and I went to the pond together.
There were just the two of us,
and all the wild things that grew
and lived in the woods.

Skunk cabbage was the first plant
we saw sprouting in the mucky, frosty mud
at the edge of the pond.

Soon the bottom of the pond thawed
in the warm spring sun.
Then big bullfrog pollywogs swam up from the mud.

Soon more frogs laid more eggs.
Salamanders did, too.
The eggs looked like balls of jelly.
There were black specks inside
the frog and salamander eggs.
These were tiny pollywogs that would soon
hatch out and wiggle around in the pond.
I saw a black and shiny salamander
with yellow spots swimming in the pond.
It looked like a little sea monster.

Tiny green duckweeds grew
on the surface of the pond.
Frogs sang, "Kerplonk!"
Each frog tried to sing louder than the others.
I thought that was funny. My father did, too.

The mallard duck and her drake
went, "Quack! Quack!" as they swam
around and around the pond together.
Soon tall swamp irises grew
at the edge of the pond in the woods.

"Look!" my father said.

I looked through his binoculars and saw three eggs
on the little island in the middle of the pond.

The mallard duck and her drake were watching over them.

"Are those eggs going to hatch
into ducklings soon?" I asked.

My father nodded his head and smiled.

Now primroses grew by the edge
of the brook that flowed into the pond.
A swallowtail butterfly fluttered in the sunshine
and sipped nectar from the primrose blossoms.

One day, the duck eggs hatched.

We could hear the ducklings if we sat very, very quietly.

Even the big bullfrogs were quiet

while the three little ducklings went,

"Cheep! Cheep!" in downy-soft voices.

"Quack! Quack!" said the duck and her drake.

When summer came, water lilies made
green circles of leaves on the still surface of the pond.
Blue and red dragonflies darted in the sunshine.
Big-eyed frogs peeked up between the water lilies.
They hung quietly in the water, looking and looking,
just like my father and me.

A painted turtle sat on a log that floated in the pond.
A little shiny sunfish swam in circles under the log.

A garter snake took a sunbath on the rocks near the place where the cattails grew.

One day, the mallard duck and her drake
and their three ducklings
swam around and around the pond.
"Quack! Quack!" the big ducks said,
and the ducklings said, "Quack! Quack!" too.

When autumn came,
the leaves on the trees
turned red and brown and gold.
Acorns and beech nuts
plopped into the pond.

Cold air made the swamp irises
bend over and die.
The frogs stopped singing, "Kerplunk! Kerplunk!"
The ducklings grew up.
They flew away with the duck and her drake
to a warm place for the winter.

Leaves fell off the trees and into the pond.
Frogs and tadpoles, salamanders, turtles,
and fish swam down and hid in the mud
for their long winter sleep.
The water lilies died in the water.
Only a few brown leaves floated
on the still surface of the pond.

White snowflakes began to fall,
for winter had come.

When the pond was frozen solid
and the woods were white with snow,
lots of people came again.
They skated on the ice
that covered the pond,
and so did my father and I.

Bag Book